HANUKKAH, OH HANUKKAH

HANUKKAH, OH HANUKKAH

Susan L. Roth

PUFFIN BOOKS

Hanukkah, oh Hanukkah,

come light the menorah.

Let's have a party,
we'll all dance the hora.

Gather round the table,

we'll give you a treat.

Dreidels to play with,

latkes to eat.

And while we are playing,

the candles are burning low.

One for each night,
they shed a sweet light,

to remind us of days long ago.

One for each night,
they shed a sweet light,

to remind us of days long ago.

HANUKKAH, OH HANUKKAH

Ha-nu-kkah, oh Ha-nu-kkah, come light the me-no-rah.

Let's have a par-ty, we'll all dance the ho-ra.

Gath-er round the ta-ble, we'll give you a treat.

Drei-dels to play with, lat-kes to eat.

To Rebecca Roth's great-grandchildren, in order of appearance:
Liat, Shira, Paul, Sophia, Lena, Max, Molly, Danielle, and Rebecca,
and all the others yet to come.

✳

Thank you to the third-grade students at Beth Tfiloh School in Baltimore, Maryland.
Many thanks also to Rona Zuckerberg, Shelly Malinow, Shoshana Krupp,
Shirley Avin, Carolyn Van Newkirk, and Zipora Schorr.
Thank you for the papers: Nobuko and Masato Kasuga, Michael Laufer, and
Jill Tarlau. And thank you to Olga R. Guartan.

✳

PUFFIN BOOKS
Published by the Penguin Group
Penguin Young Readers Group, 345 Hudson Street, New York, New York 10014, U.S.A.

Registered Offices: Penguin Books Ltd, 80 Strand, London WC2R 0RL, England

First published in the United States of America by Dial Books for Young Readers,
a division of Penguin Young Readers Group, 2004
Published by Puffin Books, a division of Penguin Young Readers Group, 2006

1 3 5 7 9 10 8 6 4 2

THE LIBRARY OF CONGRESS HAS CATALOGED THE DIAL EDITION AS FOLLOWS:
Roth, Susan L.
Hanukkah, oh Hanukkah / Susan L. Roth.
p. cm.
Summary: A family of mice celebrates the eight days of Hanukkah with friends
in this illustrated version of the holiday song.
ISBN: 0-8037-2843-3 (hardcover)
1. Children's songs—Texts. [1. Hanukkah—Songs and music. 2. Songs.] I. Title.
PZ8.3.R747Han 2004 782.42164`0268—dc22 2003013165

Puffin Books ISBN 0-14-240701-1
Manufactured in China
To make these collages, I used paste, tweezers, scissors, lace, and papers from every basket in my studio.